Colvin
and the Snake Basket

SAM McBRATNEY

Illustrated by Carol Holmes

A Magnet Book

First published in 1985
by Methuen Children's Books Ltd
This Magnet edition first published 1987
by Methuen Children's Books Ltd
11 New Fetter Lane, London EC4P 4EE
Text copyright © 1985 Sam McBratney
Illustrations copyright © 1985 Carol Holmes
Printed in Great Britain by
Richard Clay Ltd, Bungay, Suffolk

ISBN 0 416 04492 1

Contents

1 Piggy-in-the-middle

Chip chop chipper-chopper chipper-chopper chop.

Mrs Matthews sliced carrots with the big, sharp kitchen knife.

The chipper-chopper was a very important knife. Colvin had wanted to use it for a long time now.

'Mummy,' he asked, 'can this be the day I use the chipper-chopper, please?'

'No.'

'Why can't I use the chipper-chopper?'

'Because you'll slice your fingers.'

'I won't.'

'N – O spells No,' declared Colvin's big sister, Beccy, who was ten. Beccy was also slicing carrots with a very small knife.

Don't you tell me how to spell No, thought Colvin, who was beginning to get into a bad mood.

'Oh dear,' his mother said, suddenly glancing down, 'Frederick, will you stop dirtying the walls!'

Frederick was Colvin's tiny brother, who right now was standing on his wobbly legs, slapping the kitchen walls with his fat hands. Colvin noticed that Frederick did *not* stop slapping the walls, he kept right on doing it.

Colvin scowled. Lamb Chop – they sometimes called Baby Frederick 'Lamb Chop' – could do whatever he liked because he was small and Beccy

could do as she liked because she was big. I'm the only one round here who can do nothing, thought Colvin.

He said very loudly: 'I WANT TO USE THE CHIPPER-CHOPPER.'

His mother pointed the huge knife at him. It had a lovely smooth white handle.

'Colvin, if I let you use the chipper-chopper and you cut your finger...'

'He *would* cut his finger,' said Beccy.

'... People would say I was the worst Mummy in the whole street. You will *not* use the chipper-chopper and that is final.'

'You are not my friend, Mummy!' Colvin shouted. He looked serious as he walked out of the kitchen.

Upstairs in the bathroom, Colvin kicked over the straw snake basket and crawled in backwards, bringing Slippy Duck with him for company.

Slippy Duck was a plastic red and yellow duck, much more colourful than any duck who had ever lived, but he floated and he was Colvin's friend. There was plenty of room in the snake basket for Colvin and Slippy Duck and the dirty laundry – because of course, that basket wasn't for snakes at all, it just looked like a snake basket. So his father said.

I am a big snake, thought Colvin. SSSSS! Mummy had better not come near the snake basket or smart Beccy either for they'll be bitten if they do and I'll swallow Lamb Chop whole!

It was a good place to think, down there at the bottom of the snake basket. Colvin began to talk

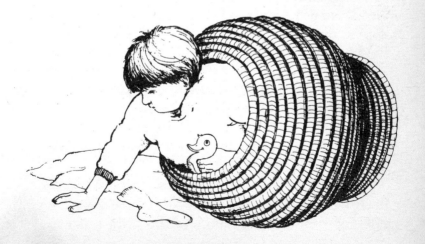

out loud. 'When I grow up,' he shouted, 'I'm going to buy *ten* chipper-choppers. Ten. I'm going to buy ten chipper-choppers of my own.'

Piggy-in-the-middle – that's what his father sometimes called him. Beccy was on top, Baby Frederick was below. Colvin was the middle child and it was a tough place to be. If anybody wanted proof they only had to think of chipper-choppers and Lamb Chop.

After a while Colvin came out of the snake basket and slid down the stairs on his bottom, bump, bump, bump. This bumping down the stairs made him think of a girl called Rosy Tea Cosy. One day in the playground he came down the slide behind Rosy Tea Cosy and zapped her right in the middle of the back with his two feet.

'Colvin Matthews,' Rosy Tea Cosy had said to him, 'you are a pillick.'

Rosy Tea Cosy called most people a pillick. Colvin didn't like her very much.

When Colvin returned to the kitchen, his sister Beccy had finished slicing the carrots. 'Look who's come back,' she said. 'Bet you were upstairs doing your snake act again.'

'I was playing with Slippy Duck, hard luck,' said Colvin, just to show how wrong she could be, 'and I'm going to buy twenty chipper-choppers when I grow up.'

'Just the right number,' said Beccy flippantly, 'one for each finger and each toe.'

Mrs Matthews giggled. She tried not to and she tried to hide it, but Colvin wasn't such a fool, he saw her shoulders moving and he didn't like it.

'Mummy,' he said, 'you are a pillick.'

Beccy froze. Her mouth hung open. 'Oh!' She was outraged. 'Oh, Colvin.' She stared at their mother, waiting for Action. 'Mummy. He called you a pillick. Didn't you *hear* him, aren't you going to *do* something?'

Mrs Matthews frowned at the pot of stew, as if annoyed that it hadn't boiled yet. 'I heard.'

'But Mummy, what ...'

'Beccy, be quiet. Colvin will tell me that he's sorry, won't you, Colvin?'

He wasn't a bit sorry. Colvin noticed that Lamb Chop had managed to get his hands into a cereal packet and had spilled some cornflakes on the floor. Those cornflakes were wasted, they would never be eaten. But nobody was cross, Lamb Chop could do what he liked.

'I'm going out to play with Lisa,' Colvin said.

'You see, Mummy – he *won't* say he's sorry!'

Turning down the stew, which had suddenly started to bubble and spit, Mrs Matthews said, 'Oh well. That's all right, Colvin, go out and play in the garden. But you are not to play with Lisa, or Justin, or Queenie, or anybody. Boys who call people names must learn.'

Colvin felt a little bit sorry, now, but he wasn't going to say so while Beccy was there because all this was her fault. Thinking that his mother wasn't the real pillick – *Beccy* was – he sniffed, and went into the garden to see his sunflowers.

All through the summer Colvin had cared for the five sunflowers which grew in the far corner of his garden beyond the Jungle Tree. They were tall and very grand looking things with long hairy legs and yellow petals. Their round faces, heavy with purple seeds now that the summer was over, had turned to follow the sun, so that Colvin found them looking over the hedge into Lisa's garden next door.

Interesting things were happening next door, Colvin heard Queenie barking. He stood on the lowest branch of the Jungle Tree to peer over.

He saw Lisa and Justin, who lived further down the street beside Rosy Tea Cosy. Lisa and Justin were playing fetch-the-stick with Lisa's dog Queenie.

'Let *go*, Queenie. Bad dog!'

Queenie had fetched the stick, but wouldn't let Lisa take it out of her mouth. This was an old problem with that dog, she chewed up sticks.

Then Queenie saw Colvin, and growled. 'Rrrrrrr – ruf!'

'Fat dog,' said Colvin.

Queenie didn't like Colvin very much, but Lisa was his best friend. 'Come over and play with us, Colvin,' she said.

'No.'

'Why not?'

'I'm not allowed to play because I called my mother a pillick.'

This news fascinated and amazed Lisa, which pleased Colvin. He loved to fascinate and amaze people, it made him feel good. Suddenly he'd turned into one of those boys who called people names. I wonder how many of us there are, thought Colvin?

Lisa said, 'But Colvin! What is a pillick? What does it look like? Is it ... is it ... *What* is it? Rosalind Cruickshanks says pillick. You shouldn't call your mother names, should he, Justin?'

Neither Lisa nor Colvin had any idea what a pillick was, so they naturally turned to their friend Justin, who was known throughout the neighbourhood as a quiet boy with brains. Some people called him 'Grandpa'. His mother was a doctor and his father went jogging at night.

'I guess it might be some kind of animal,' Justin said gravely, 'it could be almost anything. If I was you, Colvin ...'

'You're not me,' Colvin quickly pointed out.

'I know I'm not you, but if I *was* I'd say I'm sorry and then you could come over and play with Queenie.'

A voice called in the distance. 'Colvin!'

That was Daddy home! After a kangaroo jump from the Jungle Tree and a zoom along the garden path Colvin ran into the kitchen just in time to see his father lifting the lid off the simmering stew.

'Hmmm.'

'Daddy, I did the carrots,' said Beccy.

Big boaster, thought Colvin.

Baby Frederick was already strapped into his chair-with-the-tray. Mr Matthews pressed him on the nose and said, 'Hiya, button.' Lamb Chop made an ugly face.

Eventually the family sat down to eat. Mr Matthews said, 'You're very quiet today, Colvin, what's the matter with you?'

Colvin didn't answer, but Beccy did. 'Well he

wasn't allowed to use the big chipper-chopper so he got into a twist. Then he called Mummy names, he wasn't allowed to do anything except go in the garden.'

'What did he call her?'

'A pillick!'

Colvin bent his head so low that his hair almost trailed in his stew, and out of one eye he saw his mother calmly cooling a heaped spoonful for Baby Frederick.

All of a sudden Colvin felt very tight inside. What was going to happen now? Would Daddy be cross?

'Well ... what exactly *is* a pillick?' asked Mr Matthews.

'Nobody knows,' said smart Beccy. 'And he hasn't said he's sorry yet, either. Mummy says she can wait for him to say he's sorry but I think...'

'Beccy,' said Mrs Matthews quietly, 'that's enough from you.'

Colvin sat at table with his lips very tightly closed, and he felt that they were all against him. He thought it wasn't fair that he should be Piggy-in-the-Middle all the time, permanently. So he sat scowling, not looking at anybody except Baby Frederick.

He couldn't help looking at Frederick, who didn't know how to find his mouth with his spoon. He looked as though he was trying to get stew up his nose.

'Such a monkey!' said Mrs Matthews, wiping his face.

Mr Matthews left the table and returned with

more stew and a heavy red book. His fingers did some page-flicking, then he snapped the book shut. 'Well, there aren't any pillicks in the dictionary,' he announced.

'They wouldn't put a word like that in the *dictionary*, for goodness' sake!' declared Beccy, alarmed.

'But if no-one knows what a pillick is,' continued Mr Matthews, 'maybe it's not such a bad thing. Maybe it really means something quite nice.'

'Not the way Rosy Cruickshanks says it,' said Beccy.

Colvin jumped up from the table, hitching his trousers, eyes shining. 'Daddy I know what a pillick is, you bake them in the oven and they taste like pancakes, pillicks are really lovely!'

'What!' cried Beccy. Beccy drew in a deep breath so that she could say plenty more, but just at that moment Baby Frederick did a karate chop

on his dish, and sent stew flying all over the kitchen floor.

That baby just laughed, flinging stew about made him happy, but Colvin ran to help his mother to lift all the little pieces off the floor before somebody trampled on them and made a real mess.

'Thank you, Colvin,' she said when he brought some paper tissues, 'you are getting to be so sensible.' And she sneaked a quick kiss as they were kneeling together.

Goody, thought Colvin. Pillicks have been forgotten.

When bedtime came Colvin did not make a fuss as he sometimes did, he did not point out that Art and Ossie Winchester and Justin and other friends of his had mothers who allowed them to stay up late at night – he went up the stairs like a lamb, carrying the mail-order catalogue.

He liked to read the mail-order catalogue, it was his favourite book.

Colvin whipped back the curtains of his bedroom for a last look at his sunflowers, but his mother grabbed him and stuck him in bed. In a flash Colvin wrapped his arms round her neck and squeezed so hard that she had to grunt. 'Oh, Colvin, no more! I surrender.'

He laughed and laughed. 'Mummy, that's my new Neckbreaker hug, was it sore?'

'Agony. That's even worse than your Ribsquasher hug if you ask me.'

'I know!'

Colvin was very proud of his Ribsquashers and

Neckbreakers. He lifted his mother's hair, which hung round her face like a curtain, and found the ear behind it.

'I'm not going to call you any more names,' he whispered.

She tucked him in really tightly. 'That's good. Night-night.'

As soon as she'd gone, Colvin loosened his arms and brought Slippy Duck and his monkey Gus into bed for company. After feeling the weight of Mr Money Pig he opened the glossy pages of the mail-order catalogue and did some reading about toys.

2 The fearless Zippy Wam Bang

'Colvin,' said Mrs Matthews crossly, 'do you know where I found this schoolbag of yours? In the wheelbarrow in the garage! What sort of place is that to dump your schoolbag?'

Colvin, who did not like to be scolded, stood in front of his mother and sucked his top lip. Then he thought of something to say.

'Mummy, I got a star for good writing today. Miss Lynn said my letters weren't too big and they weren't too small, they were just right and I got a red one.'

He waited for praise. Colvin liked to be praised, it made him feel good.

'You also got a note, didn't you,' Mrs Matthews said in her complaining voice. 'When your teacher sends home a note you must give it to me. Lisa doesn't forget *her* notes.'

His mother's eyeballs moved as she read. 'Daddy and I have to go and see Miss Lynn this evening, she wants a chat with us.'

'About me, right?'

'All about you.'

Goody. Colvin knew about such meetings, his father called them pow-wows. Miss Lynn had put his pictures and his best writing on the wall of the classroom. He loved Miss Lynn, she was his favourite teacher. One of these days he was going to give her a Neckbreaker.

Suddenly he thought of something! Did his mother and father really understand about writing? Did they truly know how easily big fat letters squeezed the letters in between and turned them into skinny thin ones? Sometimes Colvin's writing was full of Big Fatties and Skinny Thinnies, but he was working on it.

After tea, Mrs Matthews reddened her lips in front of the mirror while Mr Matthews straightened his blue tie over her shoulder. Colvin saw them to the front door, feeling pleased that his parents had dressed up so nicely to talk about him. He liked to be talked about. Some people thought he was important.

''Bye,' shouted his mother from the car door. 'Be a good boy for Beccy.'

'Don't forget to look at Gerry Gerbil,' shouted Colvin, 'he's on the nature table.'

Colvin went inside. Beccy was too busy with her homework to talk, so he decided to go up to his bedroom. As he was bumping up the stairs backwards he heard Queenie barking in the distance.

Fat Dog wanted to play! Bending low, Colvin trailed his special monkey Gus from under the bed, and then, with a piece of rope over his shoulder, tip-toed down the stairs and into the garden.

A dangerous game was about to begin. With Queenie, Colvin was about to play a game so deadly that it could only be played when Lisa's mother and father were out. First, one end of the rope had to be tied round Gus's neck. Then Colvin carried Gus to the fence and held that monkey high so that Queenie could see him plainly.

'Rrrrrr. Wuf-wuf-wuf. Rrrr.'

'Here comes Zippy Wam Bang!' shouted Colvin.

Still holding on to one end of the rope, Colvin tossed his monkey over the hedge into Lisa's garden, and Queenie ran to get him, snarling like a jungle beast.

Not many people knew that Gus had another name. As well as plain old Gus, he became at times like these the fearless Zippy Wam Bang, Jungle Fighter. Zippy Wam Bang fought lions, crocodiles and tigers. He also liked to zap space invaders when they appeared but he never fought elephants because the elephants were his friends.

For a moment or two it seemed certain that Zippy Wam Bang would be eaten alive. He lay on the ground without making so much as a twitch while the snarling lion from next door bounded closer and closer with its teeth showing white.

Colvin waited, hardly taking time to breathe. This was the exciting bit, he could scarcely bear it!

Just when the lion thought he had Zippy Wam Bang at his mercy, Colvin heaved on the rope and brought his monkey tumbling head-over-heels across the garden with the lion in pursuit, crazy to get at him. Once again, as always, it was a close thing. Colvin lifted Zippy Wam Bang to safety in the nick of time.

He looked cheekily over the fence at Queenie. 'Fat Dog. Fat fat fat fat fat.'

Queenie panted so hard that her sides pumped in and out. She wanted that monkey so badly that she tried to jump the fence, but her dumpy little legs got tangled up in the hedge. At last she freed herself, and stood looking up at Colvin with soft, brown begging eyes. 'Throw me the monkey,' those eyes said.

Colvin did not feel one bit sorry for her. 'You will *never* get Zippy Wam Bang, lion!' he told her loudly.

Next, Colvin and his monkey climbed the Jungle Tree as far as the branch which grew over Lisa's garden. From this branch he lowered Zippy Wam Bang very, very slowly. Queenie waited below for him to come down.

At this point Colvin noticed a spectator. Lisa was watching everything he did from her bedroom window, but he didn't care.

When the monkey reached the ground, and lay still, the crafty lion acted as if nothing was happen-

ing – until Colvin gave the rope a tempting twitch.
With incredible speed, the lion suddenly dived in
for the kill – too late again! Colvin jerked the rope
and lifted Zippy Wam Bang clear.

At least, he *thought* he did. Soon he realised that
the rope felt strangely light in his hands, that it
had come off his monkey's neck, and that Queenie
already had her teeth into Gus on the ground
below!

In his whole life Colvin had never come down a
tree more quickly than he did right now. The
sound of Queenie eating his Gus terrified him so
much that he didn't even know he was shouting
out loud as he ran into his own house.

'Beccy Beccy Beccy Beccy!'

And Beccy jumped up with horror to see the
state of him. 'What? What is it!'

She didn't know what to think, and Colvin
couldn't tell her, his chest heaved and his breath
wouldn't come and his words wouldn't come,

either.

'Colvin love, what did you see?' Beccy knelt beside him. 'You'll have to tell me. I don't know what's wrong with you.'

'Qu ... Qu ... Queenie's eating my Gus!'

'Colvin! You've been playing that game again!'

Beccy snatched up the poker from the hearth, and was gone. Colvin, chasing after her, saw his sister leaping over the fence into the garden where

Queenie stood with a paw on either side of the monkey's neck.

'Grrrrr.' Fat Dog glared at Beccy's poker.

'Get away from that monkey you bad dog or I'll crack you with this poker. I will!'

But would a poker be enough? Colvin knew that Fat Dog had been waiting to get her teeth into Gus for ages – she might not give up so easily. Already there was stuffing everywhere.

'MUSH!' Beccy yelled, and swung her foot at the dog, who backed off. Swooping up Gus, she flung him over the hedge into his own garden.

The battered monkey landed at Colvin's feet. Gus had lost so much stuffing that when Colvin picked him up he felt empty.

Beccy came over the fence with her hands full of stuffing and Colvin noticed a trickle of blood on her leg. That Fat Dog had made his Beccy bleed! Boy, I'm really going to zap that Fat Dog tomorrow, thought Colvin tearfully. Nobody in the world had a sister like his Beccy, it was impossible. Colvin knew that he would love her always. He would have taken the cut off her leg and put it on his own – that's how grateful he felt. Colvin quite liked to wear sticking plasters.

They brought Gus inside and found that he had a great gash under his arm-pit and that Queenie had almost bitten off his left leg.

'Just look at him!' Beccy said as she thrust some stuffing into one of Gus's holes. 'You were playing that game again, Colvin, and you know you're not allowed. If I was you I'd be in my jammies when they all come home.'

Which couldn't be a long time away. Miss Lynn had so many parents to see that a pow-wow only lasted for twenty minutes or so. Colvin changed into his pyjamas, cleaned his teeth, and sat down-stairs with his reading book open on his knee.

He heard the car door, the garage door, the room door. Mrs Matthews smiled, and then she noticed. 'Well for heaven's sake, what on earth happened to poor *Gus?*'

Colvin sucked his top lip. Beccy said, 'We had a little accident, that's all.'

'A *little* accident? Beccy, he's coming apart!'

'He fell into Tomlinson's garden and Queenie chewed him. Daddy, we've had a tough time, we don't want any post-mortems, okay?'

The grown-up Matthews exchanged glances. 'I see. Well that's us put in our box,' said Mr Matthews.

That night, Colvin was very disappointed with his mother as she put him to bed. She didn't do any talking to him and she gave him short answers.

'Did you see Gerry Gerbil in his cage, Mummy?'

'Yes.'

'Did you like him?'

'Not much. Into bed.'

She lifted the mail-order catalogue from the covers and Colvin jumped in. 'What did Miss Lynn say about me?'

'Plenty.'

He wanted more than that. 'What like?'

'She says that you're a real livewire and I know exactly what she means, Colvin.'

Colvin didn't know what she meant. A livewire? What was that? Was that very good or just good or excellent? Maybe not even good. Colvin grabbed his mother's hair, ears and all, as she tucked him in.

'I want you to do Round-and-round-the-garden-goes-the-teddy-bear with me.'

'No. You are my disobedient boy. I do not play Round-and-round-the-garden-goes-the-teddy-bear with disobedient boys. Go to sleep, please. I'm going downstairs to see if I can fix poor Gus – it wasn't *his* fault he got eaten.'

It was Fat Dog Queenie's fault, thought Colvin. That stupid dog had made Mummy cross. Colvin slipped out of bed, got some paper and some crayons, and quickly drew a picture of yellow sunflowers with smiling faces. He fell asleep knowing that his mother would like them.

3 Raggedy-Ann

Next morning, when Beccy shuffled into the kitchen wearing a towel-turban and her bathrobe, she was singing out these words: 'Guess who I found at the bottom of the snake basket? Slippy Duck, that's who.'

Her brother Colvin did not even bother to look round, he had important things to do – like crack eggs into a bowl. This morning's breakfast

depended on him. Daddy was away to work after eating eggs which had been broken by Colvin.

But Mrs Matthews worried about Slippy Duck. 'How did he get into the snake ... I mean, the *laundry* basket?'

Colvin was much too busy to answer, and anyway, talk about Slippy Duck might lead on to talk about Gus and he did not want to talk about Gus, who had received stitches last night. Right now he was under Colvin's bed, all sewed up.

Zap! Colvin hit an egg such a wallop with a wooden spoon that egg and shell and all fell into the yellow puddle at the bottom of his bowl.

'Yukky, yukky mush!' said Beccy, peering in at Colvin's work. 'If I was an egg I'd really hate to be broken by you, Colvin.'

After breakfast Colvin called for his friend Lisa. It was a pity, he thought, that this was a no-school day because his teacher would be interested to hear that he had been eggbreaking. Miss Lynn was interested in everything that he did.

When Lisa opened the door Queenie rushed out and immediately began to nibble Colvin's shoe-laces, so he pushed Fat Dog away with his foot.

'Colvin! I saw your monkey being eaten!'

This was not something he wanted to discuss. 'Guess how many eggs I broke already,' he said, cleverly changing the subject to something he was good at, 'six. Then we ate them.'

Lisa did not appear to be properly amazed. Probably she thought eggbreaking was easy. 'I'm not coming out for a while, Colvin,' she said. 'I'm going to a competition and Luby Lou has to get ready for it.'

As soon as Lisa mentioned the word competition, Colvin decided that he should come too. He enjoyed winning competitions.

'But listen, Colvin,' Lisa explained doubtfully, 'it's a competition to find the nicest doll and it's in Rosalind Cruickshanks's garden. She's not your friend.'

Didn't matter. Any competition was better than no competition at all. 'I'll bring Justin along too,' he said.

'But Colvin, I think you need a doll to get in.'

'I'll bring a doll,' said Colvin.

He could easily bring a doll, Beccy's room was full of dolls and she didn't do anything with them now except set them up in a row every once in a while and give them marks out of ten.

I'll ask her for Raggedy-Ann, thought Colvin, she's a good one. And in exchange she can have Slippy Duck to play with in the bath, or Gus.

He went three doors down the street and called for Justin.

Raggedy-Ann was one of those no-nonsense kind of dolls who could stand up to a great deal of abuse and still come smiling through – Colvin had admired her for some years now.

Her legs could be twisted and bent and they wouldn't come off. You could bend her head over without breaking her neck. Her entire body was as red as a ripe tomato, except for her pale blue face, which was lit up by two round white eyes and by a straight, red, stitched-on smile. Most of the time she wore a plain dress of blue and white check over her tomato redness. She did not have shoes. As a matter of fact she had no ears either, but these were not missed, for Raggedy-Ann's hair covered most of her head, and this hair had the colour of sunflowers.

In her bedroom, Beccy took Raggedy-Ann on her lap and tried hard not to smile at her brother and his quaint friend, Justin.

'Are you mad? You want to enter this for a *competition*? You boys haven't got a clue.'

'But Beccy, you can play with Slippy Duck in the bath,' Colvin promised faithfully.

'Gee, Colvin – thanks!'

Flick. Beccy made Raggedy-Ann's coarse hair do a dance. 'Just look at that wig, people would rather be bald. Colvin, there's something you should know about modern dolls, they can walk, they can talk, they can make puddles. Raggedy-Ann has no chance, she'll be humiliated, Colvin, she's a *mess*. You might as well put your ridiculous chimp in for the competition.'

Colvin was not impressed by modern dolls, he had read about them in the mail-order catalogue.

'But Beccy, can I take her to the competition?'

'Take her! Take her – don't pay any attention to me, what do I know about dolls?' And with that, Beccy left the bedroom and swished the door behind her.

Colvin didn't pay any attention to Beccy. He still had a very good opinion of Raggedy-Ann, even if she wasn't perfect.

All the same, that doll needed fixing up some so that she looked good. Colvin dumped her in Justin's lap. She was his problem, too.

'She can't win looking like that, what are we going to put on her?'

Justin looked worried. People were always turning to *him* for brainwaves. 'Turkey wrapper,' he said.

'What's turkey wrapper?'

'Tin foil,' said Justin patiently. His ideas often required some explanation. 'The stuff that doesn't burn in ovens. At least she would be shiny in turkey wrapper, people would notice.'

There was turkey wrapper under the chipper-chopper drawer! In no time Colvin was down to the kitchen and back again, and soon Raggedy-Ann had a shiny new dress from her throat to her ankles. In the same drawer Colvin had come across the kitchen scissors, with which he now removed every bit of Raggedy-Ann's hair so that she was bald.

Justin's eyes really boggled. Raggedy-Ann had suddenly taken on the appearance of an old doll of ninety, and now Colvin wanted to cut off some of *his* hair and stick it on with Beccy's glue.

'No,' said Justin, 'you're not getting any.' He was not giving up any hair – hair could not be borrowed.

Colvin was disappointed. Raggedy-Ann was slowly turning into one of the best things he had ever made. He was quite prepared to beg.

'Justin.'

'What?'

'Please.'

'No.'

'But Justin, I'll zap Rosy Tea Cosy if she calls you Grandpa and if you let me have some real hair you will be safe from Rosy Tea Cosy and I'll not let her bump you out of the line in the mornings.'

This was worth thinking over. Such promises were very good value for a little hair; Justin could not ignore them. When the cutting was over he stared rather nervously at the pile of hair on Beccy's dressing-table – that pile looked immense!

But he could not deny that fascinating changes were beginning to happen to Raggedy-Ann. They plastered her yellow-spotted scalp with dollops of white glue and stuck Justin's real hair into place. Of course the top of the doll's head looked a mess after the transplant, and they saw immediately that she needed a hat. Colvin fetched a piece of pink toilet paper and wrapped it round her head like a scarf.

This was the final touch. Raggedy-Ann looked a very different lady now in her long silver dress, not to mention the pink scarf with a fringe of real human hair sticking out underneath.

'This is a bit like Cinderella, you know,' Justin said wisely.

She is going to amaze people, thought Colvin.

The new Raggedy-Ann went to the competition in a cardboard box carried on a fork-lift truck. (This was Colvin, of course, with his arms out very stiff, like prongs.)

Lisa, with Luby Lou asleep in her arms, tried to shout over the peculiar whining sound coming from the fork-lift truck as it made a left-turn in through the Cruickshanks's front gate.

'But I saw it happening, Justin!' Lisa was saying. 'Queenie got the chimpanzee in her teeth and threw it up in the air and then she bit it when it came down again.'

'How many times?'

'Hundreds, but it wasn't Queenie's fault.'

Colvin stopped whining. 'It *was* Fat Dog's fault.'

'It was *your* fault, Colvin!'

They had come by now into Rosy Tea Cosy's back garden. Colvin found himself stared at by five girls all dying to know what he had in his cardboard box.

Little Muy Ling was there. She clutched a doll from Hong Kong dressed in silky black and gold. Geraldine Elliot had wheeled a doll in a pram from three streets away.

Prams aren't fair, thought Colvin, she should be disqualified.

Rosy Tea Cosy was also present, of course, since this was her own back garden. The two other girls were strangers. They turned out to be Rosy Tea Cosy's cousins.

And that was the lot, apart from Mrs Cruickshanks and another grown-up. Colvin was disappointed – he had expected a more glorious competition than this, with a table full of prizes. He looked hard but he could not see prizes – just a thin-legged table with some cakes on top. One of the cakes had candles.

Mrs Cruickshanks met them, smiling. 'Hello, you three people. Lisa, Luby Lou looks just beautiful!'

'I crocheted her dress myself, Mrs Cruickshanks,' said Lisa, pleased.

Immediately, Colvin dipped into his box and produced Raggedy-Ann. 'I brought this. Justin and me fixed her up, she's going in for the competition.'

Mrs Cruickshanks and Lisa stared for a moment or two at a doll which was unlike anything they had seen before.

'Well for heaven's sake!' Mrs Cruickshanks declared. 'She's ... she's ... well, she's dazzling, isn't she, Lisa?'

'I don't know,' said Lisa, fascinated.

'Of course she is, she's like a fairy off a Christmas tree – but Colvin, listen.'

Mrs Cruickshanks knelt to speak quietly to Colvin, who was not surprised by her delight in Raggedy-Ann. 'You must understand that really this isn't so much of a competition, it's more of a birthday party for one of Rosalind's little cousins. Why don't you set Raggedy-Ann over there with the other dolls and I'll get you people some juice. *You* would like some juice, wouldn't you, Justin?'

Justin nodded glumly. This was the first mention he'd heard about a birthday party. There were fairly strict rules about birthday parties, and he found it embarrassing to be here without a present. It felt like cheating.

The sight of all the other dolls – six of them, had meanwhile set Colvin's tummy tingling with competition nerves. Mrs Cruickshanks was a very nice person, Colvin liked her, but she was mistaken. Those dolls weren't here for nothing. They'd come to win.

One of those dolls seemed more impressive than the others. She wore a dress of golden satin, with hat to match, and waves of white lace tumbled down her dress like running water. Justin could not resist a poke at one of the pale blue eyes of this exquisite creature – he wanted to see whether her eyeballs moved like Luby Lou's.

A voice said: 'Cut that out, Grandpa, you'll make her blind!'

Rosalind Cruickshanks had arrived. Poor Justin flushed. He felt so embarrassed to be called Grandpa in front of all these people, two of whom were complete strangers.

But help was coming. 'Rosy Tea Cosy,' said his friend Colvin, quite deliberately.

They faced each other, those two. War had broken out already. Rosalind Cruickshanks did not flinch.

'You will not call me Rosy Tea Cosy.'

'I will.'

'You won't. I'll zap you if you do.'

'You won't.'

'I will.'

This might have gone on for a long time had it not been for one of Rosy Tea Cosy's cousins, who made a startling discovery.

'Aaa!' she said. 'This doll here's wearing tin foil. Her dress is made of TIN FOIL.'

The other girls gathered round to stare. Rosy Tea Cosy turned Raggedy-Ann upside down and put dents in her dress.

'It *is* tin foil. And she's got no pants on. She's not even *dressed*!'

Colvin had no idea what to say to cover up this scandal. It was Justin who spoke up. 'That doll's got real hair, you know.'

'Whose?'

Justin seemed to grow taller. 'Mine.'

Unfortunately, just at that moment Raggedy-Ann's pink scarf floated away on a sudden little breeze and landed rather gracefully on the spikes of a gooseberry bush.

'Yaah, look at her hat!' howled Rosy Tea Cosy. 'Everybody look at her hat, it was only toilet paper.'

Even little Muy Ling dared to smile. Colvin tried to make Rosy Tea Cosy sizzle up and fry with a hot stare, but she would not be warned, she continued to howl at baldy old Raggedy-Ann in the torn, tin dress. Grabbing Raggedy-Ann by one leg, Colvin swung the doll at Rosy Tea Cosy and zapped her as hard as he could on the arm.

Some people gasped. All of a sudden Rosy Tea Cosy grew quite stiff with rage.

'Mummy!' – Mrs Cruickshanks came out of the house just then with a trayful of drinks – 'Mummy, Colvin Matthews zapped me on the arm in my own back garden.'

By now Colvin had decided that he wasn't waiting around for a drink of juice. Bundling Raggedy-Ann into her cardboard box, he took off for home. Never had a fork-lift truck been seen to move so fast, but even so, Justin passed Colvin at Rosy Tea Cosy's gate – Zoom!

I hate Rosy rotten Tea Cosy and I hate her cousins too, thought Colvin as he ran. He was also quite disappointed in little Muy Ling, who had smiled when she had no business smiling. Up until now, Muy Ling had been his friend.

When Colvin bashed open his back door and passed through the kitchen, Beccy stopped admiring herself in the hall mirror to sing up the stairs, 'Oh Mummy, *it* has returned. And I don't think it's in a good mood.'

Mrs Matthews and Beccy followed Colvin into the living-room. They did not understand that he wished to be alone. Zap! Raggedy-Ann and box were dumped in the corner.

'I hate Rosy Tea Cosy,' said Colvin.

'Well you shouldn't hate anybody,' said his mother.

'I'd like to zap Rosy Tea Cosy. I'm going to zap Rosy Tea Cosy the next time I see her.'

'There will be no zapping from you, my lad, you will zap no-one,' said his mother with her cross face on.

By now Beccy had lifted the box with her rag doll in it. 'I guess that means you didn't win. I told you, Colvin, I told you she was a tatty mess but you . . .'

But you wouldn't listen, Beccy was about to say. Then her eyes fell upon the heartbreaking sight of Raggedy-Ann, and she could not believe it.

Shreds of tattered tin foil still decorated the body of her ancient rag doll. Gone forever was her bright yellow hair – that doll was bald except for some dollops of white glue and some revolting strands of real hair off somebody's head.

'Look – what – he – has – done!'

Colvin stood behind his mother. This had not been a good day and it was getting worse. Beccy was winding herself up to shout at him.

'MUMMEEEE! Colvin, you are a pest, you are a . . . a . . . glumph! You've ruined my doll, how would you like me to cut your stupid monkey's ears off? Mummy,' she finished almost tearfully, 'why does he do these things? He's been destroying everything that's mine since the day and hour he was born.'

Such a lie! Baby Frederick was the destroyer in

the family, not him.

'You are one rascal,' his mother said. 'You had no business cutting that doll's hair off. And where did you get that hair to stick on instead?'

'It was Justin's.'

'Oh my stars!' declared Mrs Matthews.

They banished him. They sent him up the stairs and told him to feel ashamed of himself but Colvin did not feel ashamed as he kicked over the snake basket and climbed in with Gus.

With her very own mouth Beccy had said she would rather be bald than have hair like Raggedy-Ann's. I am not a destroyer, thought Colvin, I do people favours.

'Colvin.' That was his mother calling. 'Col-*vin*.'

He trailed Gus down the stairs to see what was the matter this time. Lisa had arrived with Luby Lou in her arms. Beccy was grimly fixing a new white dress on Raggedy-Ann. Mrs Matthews stood by with her arms folded in a way that made them fat. Mummy-fat-arms, thought Colvin, who was not happy.

Beccy smoothed Raggedy-Ann's new dress with one hand. 'There you are, my lovely. I'm sure you thought you were about to be cooked in that horrible tin foil. Are you coming to the wedding, Lisa? Raggedy-Ann is going to marry that monkey.'

'She's not,' said Colvin.

'She is so, it's your punishment, Colvin, so you may swallow it!'

Never, thought Colvin. Gus wasn't marrying anybody.

Happiness was bubbling up inside Lisa, she could keep silent no longer.

'Colvin, Luby Lou was second in the competition because I did my own crochet work. The judges didn't think I was old enough to do crochet work and Luby Lou got a prize.'

'Crochet work is easy,' said grumpy Colvin.

'It's not easy. Your Raggedy-Ann won a prize too, she won sweets.'

She'd won midget gems. They were sitting on the table beside a piece of tissue-wrapped birthday cake.

'Did Raggedy-Ann win first prize?'

'No, Colvin!' Lisa seemed quite shocked. 'She got a special prize for ... for ... I can't remember what for, it was a big long word.'

'Ridiculousness,' suggested Beccy.

Smart Beccy held Raggedy-Ann in front of her face and put on a false voice as if *she* was the doll talking.

'Hi there, Gus. See you at the wedding tomorrow, old bean.'

Colvin stuck his fingers in his monkey's ears. Then he picked up the packet of sweets and went into the garden with Lisa.

They sat under the Jungle Tree and did some chewing while Gus hung from a branch by his fingers. 'Colvin – Mrs Cruickshanks was cross because Rosalind laughed at your doll.'

Good. Probably Mrs Cruickshanks would like to take Rosy Tea Cosy back and get her changed for somebody better.

'Colvin.'

'What.'

'Is your chimpanzee really going to marry Raggedy-Ann?'

'No.'

4 The battle with Beccy

SLAM!

That's how Colvin shut the door of his house behind him on Monday morning, he was so keen to get to school.

By the time he reached the end of his street, he was zooming. Zoom! He zoomed past Rosy Tea Cosy and Geraldine Elliot, two slow-coaches, and as he went by he swung his plastic bag in a gigantic circle.

'What's in the bag?' shouted Rosalind Cruickshanks.

'Nosy Tea Cosy,' Colvin shouted back.

He laughed and laughed. This was going to be a great day.

When he caught up with Justin and Lisa, Colvin decided that he should stop zooming because those two people were his very good friends, and besides, he was tired zooming. That bag weighed his arm down.

Lisa noticed it immediately. 'What have you got in your supermarket bag, Colvin?' she asked pleasantly.

The bag changed hands so that Lisa couldn't peep. 'I got some news,' said Colvin.

At last he had some News for Miss Lynn. For weeks and weeks Colvin had been forced to listen to other people telling about their News. He had been convinced for a long time now that all the interesting things in life happened to other people like Ossie Winchester and Tall Norman. Ossie Winchester had been into hospital to have his crooked eye straightened and Tall Norman had lost himself in a dark picture house until a lady came with a torch and brought him back to his seat. Another good example of News was Geraldine Elliot, who brought in the bead that got stuck up her nose.

Nothing like that ever happened to Colvin, who never had News. Until now. This happy day, all that was going to change.

Miss Lynn's class lined up in the playground. All her pupils stood so tightly packed against one another that even the daylight could hardly get through – they left no spaces. There were certain people in that class who would push into the line in front of you instead of going to the end. Miss Lynn's class understood about lines.

They were excited this morning.

'Miss,' shouted Art, who was normally quite shy, 'my mum was talking to you last Friday.'

'I know she was, Arthur.'

Other people spoke up, too. '*My* mum was talking to you, Miss Lynn.'

'Miss, you told my dad I did really good work.'

All this bored Colvin. He rushed out of the line

and handed his plastic bag to his teacher. 'Miss, I've got some News for you in this bag.'

Miss Lynn opened the neck of the bag, and peered in. Her expression changed from curiosity to happy-face. 'Oh Colvin, he's gorgeous. I can't wait to hear your News about *him*. We'll keep him a secret for the time being, shall we?'

Colvin nodded happily. He loved to make his teacher smile.

Tall Norman, Rosy Tea Cosy and little Muy Ling were the lucky front three people in the line that morning. Ossie Winchester tripped Geraldine Elliot as they all marched in, but Colvin didn't laugh. That was just silly behaviour.

'On to the Talking Carpet, everyone,' Miss Lynn said loudly, 'Colvin has some News to tell us. Quietly, please.'

In one corner of the room there was a large red mat. If any talking had to be done, it was done on this carpet. People were supposed to be good when they sat on the Talking Carpet, but Ossie Winchester did a head-over-heels and Miss Lynn tapped his bottom while it was sticking up.

'Bad boys should *not* put their bottoms in the air,' she said crossly, 'now listen carefully to Colvin, we are going to write about this afterwards.'

Colvin reached into his bag and pulled out Gus by one ear. Justin recognised him immediately.

'That's the fearless Zippy Wam Bang,' he announced in a loud voice.

At the back, unlucky Lisa sat up straight to see over Tall Norman, who was such a nuisance at times like this. She could hardly believe that that

chimpanzee was still in one piece after the walloping he'd taken – bits of him had been lying all over her garden!

'He's a really lovely monkey, isn't he?' said Miss Lynn.

At teacher's feet, little Muy Ling nodded. Her eyes were bright, she loved Gus. Colvin began to tell how his monkey had been exploring in the

Jungle Tree when he was suddenly attacked by the fierce creature who lived next door. It grabbed Zippy Wam Bang with its teeth, flung him into the air and shook him until his insides were hanging out. Then help came, and he was saved.

Hardly a noise happened as Colvin told his News, he had amazed them all. Then Rosalind Cruickshanks spoke.

'I don't believe it, there are no Jungle Trees round our way.'

'It *is* true, Rosalind,' Lisa said indignantly, 'I saw it all happening.'

Heads turned eagerly to stare at Lisa. Miss Lynn sounded doubtful. 'You were there too, Lisa?'

'Yes Miss Lynn, I was watching from my bedroom window. My dog Queenie got Zippy Wam Bang and shook him until his insides were hanging out like Colvin says.'

At the front of the group Ossie Winchester piped up. Ossie Winchester always managed to get to the front of the group. 'His guts aren't hanging out now, are they?'

That remark made Colvin boil.

'Miss,' he yelled with all his might, 'Zippy Wam Bang was hurt so bad he got *stitches*.'

The class, who had been sitting like angels until now, forgot all the rules which Miss Lynn had made about good behaviour on the Talking Carpet, and rose up to see the monkey's stitches. Ossie Winchester stepped on some people and made them squeal. Sure enough, under Zippy Wam Bang's armpit where the fur was thinnest, a neat long row of stitches could plainly be seen. Colvin made sure that Rosy Tea Cosy saw them, and Ossie Winchester, too.

Miss Lynn clapped her hands and made them all sit down properly again. Then she took the monkey on her lap.

She was still curious. 'Lisa – how did Colvin's monkey get into your garden?'

'Miss, Colvin ties a rope round his neck and throws him in. Then he pulls the rope quick when Queenie comes. He's not allowed to do it but he does it.'

'Oh dear,' said Miss Lynn.

Colvin blasted Lisa with a fierce, long stare. Other people got to tell their News without interruptions like this, it wasn't fair. But Miss Lynn didn't seem to mind, she poked Gus's nose and said that he was a brave monkey to fight fierce creatures like that.

'Colvin, thank you very much for telling us such an exciting story to write about. But please stop playing that dangerous game, or he'll be destroyed, your lovely monkey.'

Miss Lynn hugged his Gus and rubbed his fuzzy fur. Colvin felt as though she were hugging *him* and he glowed with love for his teacher.

'Miss, I'm going to do you the best work ever,' he said.

There would be no Big Fat letters gobbling up the Skinny Thinnies, and his lines were going to be straight. Miss Lynn deserved the very best writing.

*   *   *

His mother was reading a story to Lamb Chop when he got home from school that day – the one about chicken-licken and turkey-lurkey and all the dumb animals who thought the sky was falling down.

Seeing those two so close together gave Colvin his Piggy-in-the-middle feeling again – that is to say, he felt jealous – but the feeling didn't last. He was a proper schoolboy now, he did his own reading. Zap! He pitched Gus into a corner of the room.

'Mummy, two stars! One for my story and one for Talking.'

'A star for talking? In class?'

She didn't understand, that's why she was amazed. 'Proper Talking, Mummy. *News*. Did Beccy ever get two stars in one day?'

'Well I don't know.'

'And Miss Lynn picked me to change Gerry Gerbil's water, I had a really great day.'

Mrs Matthews said that she had never heard the

like of it. She also made him take Gus away up the stairs where he belonged.

A short time later Beccy came home from school with her best friend Adeline Poots, who parked herself in the kitchen while Beccy ran up to change. Colvin went into the kitchen to look at Adeline Poots.

'Hiya Colvin,' she said.

'Hello.'

They didn't talk for a while. Colvin perched on a stool to see better.

'Colvin, is it true Raggedy-Ann's marrying your bear?'

'It's not a bear, Adeline,' Beccy yelled from the top of the stairs, 'it's a monkey. Actually it's a chimpanzee.'

'She's marrying a chimp! Oh that's even better. What a hoot!' Adeline Poots hooted.

'You stop laughing in our house,' Colvin told her rudely.

By now Beccy had come into the kitchen dressed in her different, more grown-up clothes, the same ones she had been wearing when she waved the poker at Fat Dog and saved Gus. She looked nice.

'Beccy, Gus isn't really getting married, is he? It's only a joke.'

'Don't be silly, Colvin, you messed up Raggedy-Ann, what else can she do with her life?'

'My Gus doesn't even like Raggedy-Ann.'

Why did Adeline Poots snigger? Colvin felt like kicking her shins.

'Colvin,' said Beccy, 'they have loved one

another for many years and you are behaving like a wicked stepfather. They are being married after tea, the guests have been invited and that is that. Goodbye.'

That's what you think, thought Colvin.

A little later in the afternoon, Colvin sneaked out the back door, climbed the Jungle Tree and left Gus hanging up there on one of the highest branches.

Beccy wasn't getting him, and neither was Raggedy-Ann.

The Matthews family had only just finished their tea when giggly-face Adeline Poots arrived at the front door.

Colvin knew why she was giggling – he was no fool, he knew why she was here. He went into the hall to say something to Adeline Poots.

'You go home, I don't want you in my house.'

'Col-*vin*,' said Mrs Matthews, who had good ear, 'that is no way to talk to Adeline. Be polite to people.'

'Be out in a minute, Adeline,' sang Beccy.

More guests arrived. This time, when the door-bell rang, Colvin found Lisa and Justin on his door-step – and Rosy Tea Cosy as well!

'I am not coming out,' Colvin told those three.

Lisa explained. 'But we're here for the wedding, Colvin, Beccy told us to come specially.'

Suddenly his hall was filling up with people! Through the partly open kitchen door Colvin noticed his mother and father listening to what was going on, and they were smiling. Then Beccy came down the stairs carrying Raggedy-Ann and that doll was wearing real daisies.

Colvin was already talking as he zapped open the kitchen door. 'Mummy, you tell Beccy Gus is mine and she can't have him.'

'I am having absolutely nothing to do with this, Colvin, it is between the pair of you.'

Beccy followed him in. 'Where have you put that monkey, Colvin? I can't find it.'

I'm not going to answer, thought Colvin. He pretended to fiddle with the toaster on the kitchen table.

'Mummy, he has hidden that monkey; Daddy, I want you to do something.'

Mrs Matthews sighed. 'Beccy...'

'Mummy it's his *punishment* for cutting off her hair and turning her into a shambles, he gets away with murder in this house.'

That was definitely not true. But Colvin did not want to speak because it was all turning into an argument. The four guests at the wedding stared in from the hall as if they were watching a programme on television, and a good one at that.

Mrs Matthews turned to Colvin. 'Where is the monkey?'

'Mummy, Raggedy-Ann can marry Slippy Duck instead.'

'Beccy' – Mrs Matthews sounded a little desperate – 'does this matter? It was only a joke.'

'Raggedy-Ann didn't look funny to me!'

Mrs Matthews glanced at her husband. She'd done enough talking. Over to you, that look said.

Daddy will be on Beccy's side because she's the

biggest, thought Colvin. But I'm not telling, I'll hide in the snake basket.

'Look, Beccy,' began Mr Matthews, 'I don't think the wedding is such a good idea, now. It's a bit...' He couldn't find a finishing word.

'I see,' said Beccy.

'Do you!' Daddy didn't sound pleased. 'Then I'd rather you didn't put on that face, it isn't necessary.'

'Always on his side,' snapped Beccy.

Mrs Matthews rose up quickly and ushered the enthralled wedding guests out of the front door, which angered Beccy still more.

'You're always on his side, those two boys get all the sympathy round here, I get none, I get nothing.'

'This is immature behaviour.'

'It *isn't*!'

'Rebecca!' Daddy roared.

Colvin left the toaster to stand by his Mother's side, for suddenly, his sister wasn't Beccy any more, she was Rebecca; and Daddy wasn't Daddy any more – he was Father.

'Grown-ups never understand anything,' Beccy began to shout, almost in tears, 'you're such a long way from my age you've forgotten everything, you don't know what it's like to be me, you have *no* idea and I might as well not exist.'

Colvin held on tightly to his mother's skirts when he heard all that coming out of Beccy's mouth. Now it was his father's turn to speak in a low, powerful voice.

'Who got half a day's pay spent on new shoes

last week? Who gets lifted and laid in the car day-in, day-out? Kids don't walk any more! Who went on a school trip to Holland last year, eh? Your Mother and I have never been out of the country. Who's got the short memory round here? Don't you talk to me like that again.'

Mrs Matthews said, 'John!'

He turned roughly to her, too. He was breathing hard. 'Some things need saying. It's best to say them.'

It is not indeed, thought Colvin, he didn't think it was a good idea to say these things and neither did Beccy. She was really crying now as she turned and ran out of the kitchen.

Colvin climbed on a stool and tugged at his mother's hair until she brought her ear down. 'Mummy, you listen to me. I'll tell where Gus is hiding and Daddy won't be cross any more.'

'Gus doesn't matter any more now, Colvin,' she answered impatiently, 'the damage is done.'

What damage did his mother mean? Suddenly he knew, it was the worst kind of damage: Daddy

didn't like Beccy any more and Beccy didn't like Daddy.

Some nasty thoughts kept Colvin awake as he lay in bed that night. Maybe Beccy didn't like *him* much, either. Maybe ... maybe she even thought that Colvin didn't like her because Gus didn't like Raggedy-Ann. He decided that he'd better go and tell Beccy he was still her friend.

The landing light was still on and Beccy's door lay partly open so the room wasn't quite dark.

'Beccy?'

'What?'

She was awake. Colvin pulled back the covers and jumped into the warm beside her. Then he whispered. 'Beccy, I don't like Daddy when he shouts, I like you better.'

She didn't answer. Colvin put an arm round her and gave her a very gentle Ribsquasher. Of course there was really no such thing as a very gentle Ribsquasher, but this was a special occasion.

'Beccy, are you still my friend?'

Maybe she wasn't! She didn't answer him immediately. 'Yes, Colvin, I'm still your friend. You'd better go back to your own bed or he'll shout at you, too.'

Colvin slipped out of bed, then ran back from the door to whisper something else.

'If you want to know where Gus is, he's up the Jungle Tree. I think he would like to marry Raggedy-Ann.'

Colvin jumped into his own bed thinking how this was a truly awful lie, but some things were more important than monkeys.

5 The dreadful Minty

When Daddy came home from work the next day Beccy jumped into his arms and they exchanged Ribsquashers and Colvin was happy to see that they liked one another once more.

Also, Daddy bent down and kissed Lamb Chop's top-of-head. Baby Frederick was obviously too young for a good Ribsquasher, which would break up all his small bones. Colvin was having a think about that problem when his mother came through the back door holding Gus by one ear. That monkey wasn't just wet, he dripped like a sponge.

'Guess who I found at the bottom of the Jungle Tree! Left out all night if you please – in the pouring rain!'

Poor Gus was a soggy sight. Colvin hadn't

remembered another thing about him, this was another good example of how his memory had holes in it.

'Colvin, I am sick and tired of this monkey. Run up and set him in the bath beside what's-his-name.'

'Slippy Duck,' said helpful Beccy.

As Colvin ran up the stairs with the still-dripping Gus he heard the rest of his family hooting in the kitchen. They were happy again.

After tea Mrs Matthews plonked Colvin on her lap and opened his reading book. It was homework time.

'Mummy,' said Colvin, 'will I read you the mail-order catalogue instead?'

'You will not, you will read me a proper book. Start!'

He was a prisoner. So he began to read, and when he came to a word which was obviously too long for a person of his age he poked his mother with his elbow.

The story was about a boy called Ginger. Ginger wasn't his real name, they called him that because of the colour of his hair. Colvin stopped reading to ask a question.

'Mummy?'

'What is it?'

'Who hands out the extra names?'

Mrs Matthews tapped the reading book. 'Colvin, I don't know what you are talking about. What kind of extra names do you mean?'

'He means nick-names,' said smart Beccy. 'They just get stuck on you.'

'*Read!*' said Mrs Matthews.

Colvin read some more. Then he began to think of names like Lamb Chop and Rosy Tea Cosy – even Justin had an extra name. Colvin had no idea why people called him Grandpa, it was one of those mysterious things. You got a name in Church when you were new and then, sometimes, you got another one. But who handed out the extra names?

'I'd like an extra name,' Colvin suddenly said.

'How about Nyerp?' answered smart Beccy.

I'll give myself an extra name, thought Colvin. Was such a thing possible? It made him fidget with excitement on his mother's knee just to think about it.

Mrs Matthews had come to the end of her rope – she was getting angry. 'Right, everybody out of here. You too, Sleeping Beauty' – this was Daddy, who woke up to find Lamb Chop laughing on his knee – 'Colvin needs peace to do his reading properly and we cannot have all these distractions.'

Colvin liked distractions, they were more fun than reading. But he sat up good because a very interesting idea had just occurred to him.

Tomorrow, he thought, I'll give myself an extra name. I'll be somebody else as well as myself.

Next day, Colvin and Lisa and Justin walked home from school through the park because Justin had some crusts left over from his lunch and he wanted to feed them to the Town Ducks.

The Ducks of the Town lived on a shallow,

shiny pond in the centre of the park. When they saw Justin, two dozen beaks headed in his direction. The Town Ducks knew Justin was their friend.

After watching a few duck-fights, Colvin decided that now was a good time to let out his secret.

'I've got a new name,' he said to his friends, 'from now on people have to call me Minty. Colvin Matthews and Minty Matthews – that's me.'

This news didn't bother Justin, who continued to divide the crusts of his sandwiches into small pieces suitable for duck beaks. Justin was not easily amazed.

But Lisa was very different. 'Minty? *Minty?* When did you get the name Minty?'

'I gave it to myself at lunchtime.'

Lisa frowned, as if this was a very fishy business.

'Justin,' said Colvin, 'say Hello to me using my extra name.'

'Hello, Minty.'

Colvin was satisfied. He felt like a Minty. Now it was Lisa's turn.

'Say Hello to me using my extra name.'

That frown hadn't gone away from Lisa's forehead, something still bothered her.

'You've always been Colvin,' she reminded him, 'I don't see how you can be Minty as well as Colvin.'

'Well I'm Minty now!'

'All right then,' said Lisa, just as loudly. If Colvin Matthews wanted to sound like a polo mint that was his business. 'Hello *Minty.*'

Satisfied, Colvin slung some bread crumbs to the Town Ducks. His extra name had made quite a good start, soon Ossie Winchester and Tall Norman and little Muy Ling would be calling him Minty, too. Having an extra name was fun; he felt different.

On the way home Colvin and Lisa and Justin stood under the railway bridge to listen for trains coming. They liked to hear the wheels of a train passing over the top because it felt like you were being crushed by the rumble-thunder noise.

Lisa noticed something. 'This bridge has been written on by bad boys.'

Squiggles and names covered the inside walls of the bridge. It looked ugly.

'*And* girls,' said Justin.

'Justin, girls do not write on bridges.'

Justin didn't argue. It was enough for him to know that he was right.

Some of the names which Colvin read on the cement slabs certainly had not been handed out in Church, they were extra names. Like Minty. Maybe, thought Colvin – and this was an exciting thought – maybe Minty could do some interesting things which Colvin would be afraid to do. Minty felt different from Colvin, and he might easily write his name up on the railway bridge in big black squiggly letters.

I am *Minty*, thought Colvin.

As soon as Colvin got home from school he changed into his old clothes and began to rummage through his boxes of used toys until he found some left-over pieces of coloured chalk among the junk. Joyfully thrusting these into his pockets, he ran to call for Lisa and Justin.

Justin remembered. He said, 'Hiya Minty.'

'Colvin,' said Lisa, 'your hands are all red, what have you been doing?'

'I got chalk, look. We're going to do some writing.'

'Where is your blackboard?'

Lisa didn't understand. The new Minty Matthews didn't need a blackboard for his chalk, he bent right down and wrote MINTY in big, big yellow letters on the pavement, right at Lisa's toes. This was the biggest writing Colvin had ever done – when he measured those letters against his feet, they were bigger than his shoes.

Even Justin was amazed. His eyebrows went up.

Fascinated, Lisa and Justin followed Colvin down the road a little way to a lamp-post on which

he wrote KING MINTY gloriously in red. Then he stopped at the wall in front of Rosalind Cruickshanks's house and picked out his largest piece of white chalk.

'Justin.'

'What?'

'How do you spell Tea Cosy?'

While Justin did the spelling, Colvin wrote ROSY TEA COSY in huge white letters on Rosalind Cruickshanks's wall, and when he had finished he made the whole thing prettier still by filling in the O in ROSY with green, and the O in COSY with red.

Next, Colvin wrote JUSTIN on the kerbstone in yellow. He wished he had some blue-coloured chalk. He really missed not having blue.

Meanwhile, Justin was absolutely horrified to see his name written so prominently on the public pavement. This was not his idea of good fun, he did *not* want his name down there.

'I want you to rub that out,' he said.

'Why?'

'People will walk over it.'

'I don't care,' said Colvin. And he kicked Justin when Justin tried to rub out the letters with his foot.

Justin, quietly puzzled by this new Colvin who no longer cared about him, decided that it was time he went back to his own house. It was quite obvious to Lisa that he was sad because Colvin had been nasty to him.

'Justin has gone home because of you, Colvin. He doesn't like you any more.'

'I don't care,' said Colvin.

To show how little he cared, he reached into Mrs Webster's garden and wrote MINTY on the smooth bark of her ornamental cherry tree. Underneath in green he drew a small picture of Slippy Duck, adding a cute little beak with his last bit of yellow chalk. When he looked round to check what Lisa thought of this piece of work, he found that Lisa had gone home, too.

Still, Colvin did not care. Right now he was Minty, a different person than he used to be, and he was going to keep on writing and writing until he had no chalk left.

Drring-drring. Drring-drring. The telephone sounded off in Mrs Matthews's hall, demanding to be answered. Beccy got to it first.

'It's all right, Mummy,' she hollered up the stairs, 'that'll be Adeline for me.' And she sang into the mouthpiece, 'Hello-oo.'

In a very short time Beccy learned that the person on the other end of the line was not her friend Adeline and she was sorry she'd been in such a hurry to grab the phone, for this was Mrs Webster from round the block and she had some pretty incredible information.

In fact it was so incredible that Beccy wondered out loud whether Mrs Webster had made some kind of mistake.

'But are you sure it's our Colvin, Mrs Webster?' she pleasantly inquired.

Of course it was Colvin, there was only one Colvin! And he had written on her beautiful cherry tree and made perfectly horrid little squiggly drawings on it in green chalk. Beccy had to listen for quite a while to Mrs Webster talking about her Colvin.

She felt so ashamed to be his *sister.*

'I'll tell Mummy at once, Mrs Webster,' she promised.

Beccy stuck down the phone.

'*Mummeeee!*' She felt entitled to yell, this was an emergency. Mrs Matthews poked her head over the landing bannister.

'For goodness' sake Beccy, such a racket. Anybody would think you were in agony.'

'Mummy, Colvin wrote on Mrs Webster's cherry tree, that was her on the phone, she's complaining about him.'

Tut-tutting sounds came from upstairs. 'Such a fuss about nothing. Beccy, go round there and clean up her cherry tree.'

'But it's not just her cherry tree' – her mother didn't understand – 'Mummy he's writing everywhere, he's writing all over the neighbourhood in four different colours of chalk!'

Beccy heard those familiar words 'Oh my stars!' Her mother appeared on the stairs, but only briefly, for she was in a hurry now, and did she look angry! 'Mind Frederick for me Beccy, there's a pet, I am going to murder that other rascal.'

Zoom, slam, she was gone. Gee, I'd hate to be Colvin, thought Beccy.

Mrs Matthews had scarcely taken a few determined strides away from her own house before she noticed the first of the changes which her son had made to the neighbourhood. On the pavement it said MINTY in yellow. On a lamp-post it said KING MINTY in red. She saw ROSY TEA COSY written in white with the circles coloured in. She read I AM KING MINTY in a mixture of red and white and green.

Then she saw him. He was squatting over a manhole cover, making pretty patterns with the last few stubs of his coloured chalks.

'Col-*vin*!' Colvin jumped to his feet, horror in his eyes. 'What do you think you are doing?'

He tried to think. But he did not get a chance to think long. His mother was only starting. 'Get into the house, I am mortified. Writing on people's fences, what has got into you? Oh! You will never have chalk in your hand again, my lad, as long as you live. What am I going to say to Mrs Webster if she ever speaks to me again? Your baby brother has more sense than you have, you bad *rascal*!'

Lamb Chop can't even write, thought Colvin, but this was big trouble.

'Mummy, it wasn't really me, it was Minty.'

'I am going to Minty you when I get you back to the house. Hurry *up*!'

She grabbed his arm and hauled so hard that he had to run to keep up. When he came through the back door Beccy was sitting with Frederick on her knee.

'Hooligan.'

'Mummy, tell Beccy she's not to talk to me.'

'Cherry tree vandal,' cried Beccy.

Colvin pushed himself into a corner and stood scowling at the floor while his mother filled a small bucket with soapy suds.

'Beccy,' she called over one shoulder, 'take Frederick into the other room, I want to speak to Colvin alone.'

'He's a problem child,' Beccy warned her mother, going out.

Colvin, thumb in mouth, glared at her. Zap! his eyes said.

Swish and plonk. The bucket appeared at his nose. 'You will take this water and wash off all that chalk.'

'I will,' said Colvin.

'Now tell me – who is this Minty person?'

'I made him up. He was my extra name, I didn't want to be just Colvin.'

'What's wrong with being Colvin?'

Colvin was ready to talk – talking might help to rescue him. 'Minty does brave things, Mummy. He's clever like Beccy and he's fierce like Ossie Winchester.'

His mother looked at him for a long time with her thinking face on. 'Listen,' she said, 'I don't want you to be as fierce as Ossie Winchester and you are every bit as clever as Beccy. Colvin my love, nobody wants you to change. Miss Lynn said her class would be dull without her Colvin, you make the whole class smile. Everybody likes Colvin and this Minty person is going to disappear.'

His mother was forgetting somebody. 'I don't think Rosy Tea Cosy does.'

'Stop calling her Rosy Tea Cosy, then. Now run out with this bucket and clean up the awful mess you made and no more of your nonsense.'

Colvin enjoyed carrying the bucket of sloppy water, it made him feel like a window-cleaner as he walked slowly up Justin's path. He wished he had a ladder, he admired all window-cleaners.

The bell was too high for him to reach, so he rattled the letter-box until Justin showed up in his socks. 'Justin, are you coming out to play with me.'

'No.'

'I got some water here.'

The pail of water jiggled and some lively drops escaped on to Justin's front step. Of course Justin was curious, but he still had his doubts. Colvin had offended him very deeply.

'You wrote my name on the pavement.'

'No! That was Minty. Minty's dead,' Colvin said happily, 'I zapped him.'

Justin was glad to hear that the dreadful Minty had been zapped. It was safe to come out.

'Well all right. I'll get my wellies.'

6 Come out of the snake basket, Colvin

When Mr Matthews came into the kitchen on Friday morning he got the biggest shock of the week so far. Colvin was standing there with a giant sunflower in his hand.

It looked like a monster which had just wandered in from the garden. The yellow petals almost brushed the ceiling.

Said Mr Matthews: 'What? Am I in the wrong room? Is this a greenhouse?'

Colvin squirmed in his pyjamas with pleasure. 'Daddy, I cut down one of my *sunflowers*.'

The biggest one. The one with the hairiest leg and the biggest top. Just one chop and the sunflower had surrendered.

Mrs Matthews took pity and did some explaining to her husband. 'From what I can gather, the sunflower is going to school today.'

'*All* of it?'

'All of it,' said Beccy. 'Miss Lynn is going to put it in a jar of water.'

Colvin was delighted. He had amazed his whole family except for Lamb Chop (who didn't understand these things), and he loved to amaze people. He smiled until his mouth wouldn't stretch any more.

'Daddy, it's for food.'

'Ah! Miss Lynn *eats* sunflowers.'

'No, it's for Gerry Gerbil!'

Of course, nobody in his family really understood about Gerry Gerbil, so Colvin had to explain while they ate breakfast.

Gerry Gerbil lived in a small cage which sat on Miss Lynn's Nature Table. He was a lovely little white creature about the size of a large mouse and he owned a long, whippy tail that looked like a worm.

'Yukky yuk,' said Beccy. Colvin kept on talking, he was getting to the important bit.

During the holidays, and sometimes at weekends, Miss Lynn allowed a sensible person to take Gerry Gerbil home in his cage, and look after him. There would be no school next Monday and Tuesday, so this Friday – today – Miss Lynn would pick someone to look after Gerry Gerbil for four whole days.

This was no ordinary day. The person who looked after Gerry Gerbil was a very important person. 'Miss Lynn will probably pick me,' Colvin finished confidently, 'I'll be coming home with Gerry Gerbil in his cage. You'll say he's nice,

Mummy.'

Mrs Matthews seemed doubtful. 'I'm sure Gerry Gerbil is adorable,' she said, 'but Colvin – why will Miss Lynn pick you? Do none of her other children want to take him for his holidays? What about Art, and Justin, and Rosalind?'

Mention of Rosy Tea Cosy made Colvin scowl. He definitely did not want her to get Gerry Gerbil, that would be the worst thing.

'Everybody wants to take him home, but they haven't got sunflowers like me. Gerry Gerbil loves sunflowers, he cracks the seeds open with his teeth.'

His family looked at the giant flower propped against the fridge. They understood completely.

'Clever, clever!' said Beccy.

They were so busy looking at the sunflower, and chatting about it, that they forgot to keep an eye on the clock. Suddenly the Matthews family began to buzz when they saw what time it was. Colvin flew up the stairs to fling his jammies off and get his clothes on – he did not want to start off this important day by coming in *late*.

In the hall his mother made his hair neat by licking her fingers and sticking down his springy-up bits. Colvin did not like his hair stuck down with lick, but he did not complain. This was not a complaining day.

He said, 'I'm going to be really good in school today.'

'I hope you're good in school every day, Mister.'

'I am. Today I'm going to be best.'

His mother's face looked thoughtful as she straightened his tie. 'Colvin – Miss Lynn might not pick you to look after Gerry Gerbil, so you mustn't get too built-up on that. She's got other children in her class, you know.'

'Twenty-eight more, but I think she'll probably pick me.' And Colvin marched off to school with his six-foot sunflower sticking in the air.

On the way to school that morning Colvin soon had lots of company. Lisa came skipping and Justin came running as soon as they spotted him, and of course, he wasn't hard to spot. Art made his father stop the car so that he could follow the other people who were following Colvin's sunflower to

school. A double-decker bus driver tooted his horn and passengers stared out of the windows of his bus. Each face, one after another, was amazed.

I amazed a whole bus! thought Colvin.

When the time came to form a neat line in the playground, he quickly found himself a place quite near the front and stood on his best behaviour.

It was important not to be seen pushing on this particular day.

The line that morning was not a particularly good one, it bulged a bit in the middle because of the curious people who twisted to stare up at the sunflower above all their heads. Then Rosalind Cruickshanks appeared. Instead of taking the last place in the line she marched half-way up it, stuck in her shoulder, wriggled a bit – and two unfortunate people popped out of the line on the other side.

Those two people happened to be Justin Clarke and Colvin Matthews.

Justin did the sensible thing, and walked to the back of the line. If there was Trouble Rosalind Cruickshanks would embarrass him by calling him Grandpa.

In his heart, Colvin did not want Trouble, either. On the other hand he knew that nobody – except for Justin – *nobody* gave up his place in the line without a fight.

Besides, a tragic thing had happened because of what Rosalind Cruickshanks did. His sunflower had been broken. Little Muy Ling nearly died when she saw its fine yellow head hanging miserably down.

Colvin thought very seriously for a moment or two. 'You broke my sunflower's leg, Rosy Tea Cosy,' he said. Then he swung his schoolbag and zapped her as hard as he could.

Immediately, Rosalind Cruickshanks opened her mouth and let go a wail which reached the distant boundaries of the playground and made Ossie Winchester stick his fingers in his ears. Of course by this time Miss Lynn's line had broken up so completely that it didn't look like a line at all any more, it was just a mass of bodies pushing and shoving to see better; until Miss Lynn arrived looking so fierce that all the loose bodies scrambled to get back into a decent line again.

Miss Lynn said in her crossest voice, 'I thought all you people had learned to be sensible!'

The entire class fell silent, except for Rosalind. 'Miss Lynn. Uh-uh-uh' – that was her breathing between sobs – 'Miss, Colvin Matthews hit me with his schoolbag and it's really sore.'

Colvin stood to one side, out of the line, alone, scowling, with his broken sunflower in his hand. 'There is *no* hitting in my class. I do not allow hitting and I don't mind telling you, Colvin, that I am extremely disappointed with you.'

She wasn't the only one. She could not know how disappointed Colvin was with himself.

'Miss Lynn?' Lisa spoke up nervously, but with great determination. 'It wasn't just Colvin's fault. Rosalind bumped him out of the line and he wasn't the only one. Justin was bumped too, weren't you, Justin?'

Safely tucked away at the back of the line, Justin did not want to be involved in stupid arguments. He decided that his lace needed tying, so he tied it.

Miss Lynn sighed, and looked round the playground. Every other line had already gone into school, they were the very last.

'Colvin and Rosalind, you two bad people go to the back of the line and come in last. Let us hope that we are not going to have one of *those* days.'

Inside, settled at his table, Colvin realised that he had better do something good. His day hadn't started too well. Right now was the time to get it out of his teacher's head that Colvin was this Friday's trouble-maker, or he would never be picked to bring Gerry Gerbil home.

So he held up his broken sunflower. 'Miss, look what I brought in. Food for Gerry Gerbil. This sunflower's got good seeds in it.'

At last, Miss Lynn smiled at him. Colvin was so pleased to see that she was his friend again that he wanted to get up out of his seat and give her a good Ribsquasher.

What a pity she hadn't seen his sunflower before its leg had been broken by Nosy Rosy rotten Tea Cosy.

In the morning time everybody worked hard for Miss Lynn and Colvin knew the reason why. They were all craftily trying to be good so that they would get Gerry Gerbil home.

In the afternoon they did measuring in groups. They didn't have to measure little tiddly things, they got to measure real people, and this was great fun – especially if you happened to get in the same group as Tall Norman who really knew how to grow.

Lisa, Art, and Justin were in Colvin's group for measuring and they decided that Colvin should be measured first because he was the smallest person and therefore the easiest to do.

'But you'll have to take your shoes off, Colvin,' said Lisa.

'No. I'm not taking my shoes off, we didn't take our shoes off last time.'

Justin nodded wisely. 'We did.'

And Art said, 'We did. I had a hole in my sock.'

So Colvin took off his shoes, set them neatly to one side, and stood against the wall to be measured. Art put a mark on the wall where his head stopped and Lisa measured from the floor.

'You are one hundred and ... six centimetres.'

Good, that sounded plenty. 'What was I last time?'

Lisa glanced at the sheet with all the heights written on it.

'One hundred and six centimetres. You haven't grown any, Colvin.'

He absolutely refused to believe it! Was he stuck on one hundred and six centimetres for ever? 'I want Justin to measure me,' he said loudly.

So they made a fresh mark, and Justin did the measuring. This time they got one hundred and eight centimetres.

'See? I knew I'd grown some.' Colvin was relieved as he looked for his shoes.

But where was his left shoe? It wasn't where he

had put it – beside his right one.

Somebody had pinched his shoe in broad daylight! Somebody wanted him to walk about the classroom with one shoe on and one shoe off, but who was it?

First he thought it must be Rosy Tea Cosy, but she seemed to have her hands full measuring Tall Norman. (People were claiming he'd grown four whole centimetres.) Colvin had just decided to blame Ossie Winchester when he saw the heel of his shoe sticking out of little Muy Ling's schoolbag.

Colvin failed to notice something as he snatched his shoe from Muy Ling's bag. He was so busy pulling on his shoe that he didn't see how he had spilled Muy Ling's egg sandwiches over the classroom floor. The first he knew about his mistake was when Geraldine Elliot's voice piped up: 'You've got egg on your socks, Norman.'

Tall Norman glared all the way down. How dare somebody put egg on his socks!

But he wasn't the only one. Other people had

trampled on the sandwiches, some with shoes on and some with shoes off, and they had spread tiny bits of yellow yolk all over the floor.

Poor Muy Ling was horrified to see that some of her bread had been mushed into Miss Lynn's lovely Talking Carpet. It was awful.

'Miss,' Geraldine Elliot said importantly, 'people are walking on Muy Ling's sandwiches.'

Miss Lynn closed her eyes, as if she hoped that the mess would somehow go away by itself. Lisa put an arm round the shoulder of Muy Ling, who had begun to cry, and all those who sniffed got an eggy smell up their noses.

'Oh no,' groaned Miss Lynn. 'Look, stand still, everyone. Justin! – you go to the caretaker this minute and bring me a brush. Muy Ling, *why* do you bring millions of sandwiches to school if you're not going to eat them? And stop crying, I know it wasn't your fault. Whose fault was it? Who was fiddling with Muy Ling's schoolbag?'

Colvin was. Several people said it. Anyway, his faced showed clearly that he was the guilty one. Colvin wanted to explain about his missing shoe, but his teacher had no time for explanations.

'Colvin, please go and stand-out by the door. No, don't give me any excuses, you shouldn't have been near another person's bag.'

'But Miss, my shoe . . .'

'Colvin!'

Quietened and sad, Colvin did as he was told. Some people like Ossie Winchester thought it was funny to see Colvin stood-out, but *he* didn't think it was funny.

He was beginning to hate this Friday.

In a few minutes, when the room had been tidied up, Miss Lynn allowed Colvin to return to his seat. Like everyone else he sat up straight and good, for Miss Lynn had lifted Gerry Gerbil's cage from the Nature Table on to her desk.

It was time!

Who would get him? The class was so quiet that everyone could hear Ossie Winchester sniffing.

'Now then,' said Miss Lynn, 'we have to pick a sensible person to look after jolly Gerry Gerbil until next Wednesday. Gerry Gerbil likes to go on his holidays too, you know.'

Hands flashed upwards. Colvin came out of his seat in an effort to get his hand every bit as high and every bit as noticeable as Tall Norman's. Some people forgot the rules and shouted out.

'Miss Lynn it's my turn!'

'It's not your turn, Art.'

'I'm sensible, Miss,' shouted Ossie Winchester.

You are not! thought Colvin fiercely. Ossie Winchester has no sense.

'*I'm* a very sensible person, Miss Lynn,' said Rosalind Cruickshanks nicely.

This was more than Colvin could bear. 'You're not sensible,' he shouted at the top of his voice, 'and you haven't got sunflowers!'

Miss Lynn put an end to all the wild talk. 'Lisa – would you like to take Gerry Gerbil home for his holidays?'

Lisa was so pleased to be the chosen person that she didn't speak, she just sat with her eyes glowing while everyone looked at her and thought how she was the lucky one to be in charge of Gerry Gerbil.

Colvin was glad when the school bell rang.

On the way home from school Lisa had more helpers than she wanted, including Tall Norman, Rosalind Cruickshanks, little Muy Ling and her very good friend Justin.

'Look,' Lisa said, shifting the cage from her right hand to her left, 'I can carry Gerry Gerbil all by myself, thank you very much.'

A little way behind this bunch of people came Colvin. Now and then he kicked a stone as hard as he could kick.

Soon Lisa reached her front gate, by which time all her helpers had gone home except for Justin and Colvin.

Mrs Tomlinson was pruning roses in the garden. 'Mummy! Look who I've got! I have to look after him until next Wednesday, isn't he gorgeous?'

Mrs Tomlinson did not say that the pinky-white little creature in the cage was gorgeous. She couldn't help noticing its red eyes, its tiny spiky feet, and the long tail which slithered across the floor of the cage like a worm.

'Oh Lisa, it looks like a rat, it really does.'

'Well he's not a rat, Mummy, he's Gerry Gerbil and he's home for his holidays. Isn't that right, Colvin?'

No reply came from Colvin, because he wasn't there any more.

He was in a foul mood as he zapped open the kitchen door with his shoulder. Then he dumped his schoolbag in the middle of the kitchen floor as if he would never need that schoolbag again.

'I don't like school any more!' he shouted at his mother.

That schoolbag lying on the floor made Mrs Matthews arch her eyebrows rather dangerously, but she calmly reached into the fridge and set out two yogurts – one for him and one for Beccy who would be in shortly.

Lamb Chop had already eaten his yogurt, his chubby face was plastered with yogurt. Yogurt-face, thought Colvin. While some people had to go to places like school, that baby stayed home and ate yogurt all day.

His mother spoke. 'Well. You didn't get Gerry Gerbil home with you, then.'

She looked as though she might try to comfort him, but he didn't want comforting and he didn't want yogurt, he wanted to feel cheated, miserable and nasty.

'No I didn't. I zapped Rosy Tea Cosy, I spilled sandwiches, I got stood-out and I didn't get Gerry Gerbil. I don't care.'

He said all that as if he was proud of all the bad things he had done, then he went upstairs to the snake basket, which was the proper place for feeling cheated, miserable and nasty.

It was full to the brim with dirty laundry, but that didn't matter to Colvin, who swiftly kicked it over, scooped out some clothes to make room, and crawled in backwards. Inside, he swayed about until the basket stood upright.

I'm not going back to school, thought Colvin, I'll stay at home and read the mail-order catalogue. He covered his head with dirty socks so that he was sitting in the snake basket in the dark.

It was quite obvious to him now that his teacher didn't care how he felt, it didn't matter that he'd brought in a whole sunflower, she liked good people who didn't zap Rosy Tea Cosy and who didn't spill sandwiches. Miss Lynn was cruel, it was all cruel. Colvin sat in the snake basket until he cried, and tasted hot spicy tears in his mouth.

After what seemed like a long while he heard steps coming to the top of the stairs, where they turned left. He kept very still so that the basket wouldn't creak.

It was Beccy.

'Come out of there, Colvin, that's the stupidest place to hide anybody ever thought of.'

'I don't want you to talk to me,' said Colvin. His voice sounded muffled.

Beccy lifted the dirty socks and found him. 'You've been crying.'

'I *haven't.*'

'Colvin, come on, I know exactly how you feel.'

How could she? None of her teachers had ever kept a Gerry Gerbil.

'Colvin, I'll tell you a secret if you come out of the snake basket. You love secrets, I know you do.'

It was true, he loved secrets. 'What?'

'You remember Adeline beat me by just one mark in the Girl's Brigade exam? Well she cheated, Colvin. She cheated in the Scripture exam, can you imagine anything worse? I was so disappointed, just like you are over Gerry Gerbil. Life is very full of disappointments, Colvin. Show me how you get out of the snake basket.'

'You know how to get out of the snake basket,' said the muffled voice.

'I don't Colvin, honestly, I know how you get in but I don't know how you get out.'

Getting out of the snake basket wasn't easy, it was dangerous. Colvin could understand why Beccy would like to see how it was done.

'Okay, are you watching? I'm coming out.'

Inside the basket, Colvin began to sway his body from side to side. As he swayed the basket began to rock ... and rock ... and rock. Suddenly it rocked too far and toppled right over.

Colvin crawled out, laughing. He could see that Beccy was amazed.

'Aren't you ever hurt?'

'No! I do it all the time.'

Beccy put an arm round him and talked some more about Gerry Gerbil, but Colvin didn't listen. He had decided that he wasn't going to visit that gerbil in Lisa's house and he wasn't going to waste his good sunflowers by giving it food, either, Lisa would have to feed it all by herself.

I don't like Gerry Gerbil any more, Colvin thought cheerfully.

7 Another Gerry Gerbil

On Monday morning, Colvin decided to be Gerry Gerbil's friend again.

This is what he did. He got up early in the morning at a quarter past eight and sneaked the large chipper-chopper out of the kitchen drawer. Then, wearing his pyjamas and his wellington boots, he went down to the corner of the garden where his sunflowers grew.

Chip chop chipper-chopper chipper-chopper chop. As Colvin had always suspected, using the

chipper-chopper was easy. One of his sunflowers fell right over, and he cut off its lovely yellow head with two more mighty chops.

That head was packed with good seeds. Colvin carried it indoors.

Beccy was so busy feeding Lamb Chop one of his special little meals out of a jar that it was easy for Colvin to slip the sharp big knife into the drawer where it stayed.

'I saw you, Colvin,' said Beccy.

Colvin spun round, sticking out his chin defiantly. 'You didn't.'

'I *saw* you, Colvin, you must think people are blind. You sneaked the chipper-chopper out ot the drawer and you cut down that sunflower with it and you are really for it if I tell Mummy.'

Suddenly life was not so enjoyable. His sister was a rotten spy.

'Mummy won't like you if you tell tales on me.'

'Mummy won't like *you* for stealing the chipper-chopper, Colvin, you didn't even wash it. The stems of those flowers might be deadly poisonous for all you know – they look it, the big hairy things.'

Beccy is poisonous, thought Colvin.

At that moment Mrs Matthews came into the kitchen with tatty hair and a dressing-gown on and floppy slippers on her feet. She kissed Beccy and swooped on Baby Frederick.

'Good morning, my sweet little Lamb Chop,' she said, 'aren't you the lucky boy with a big sister who can feed you while your lazy mummy lies in her bed!'

Huh, thought Colvin jealously. Feeding Lamb Chop was easy, anybody could feed Lamb Chop, the only person who couldn't feed Lamb Chop was Lamb Chop himself.

'Something you should know, Mummy,' Beccy said. 'Colvin used the chipper-chopper to cut down his sunflower.'

The look which Colvin threw at Beccy was a chilly one indeed. He certainly let her know that he wasn't her friend and that he never would be.

'Will I do the toast?' Colvin said very loudly.

Mrs Matthews had absolutely no interest in toast. It was Colvin who interested her right now.

'Did you? Did you use that chipper-chopper?'

'Mummy...'

'Now you listen to me, my boy. I do *not* like disobedient children. Some day you will make a mistake with that chipper-chopper and slice your fingers open.'

'And lose all your blood,' said smart Beccy, 'you've only got eight milk bottles full.'

Eight milk bottles full? Colvin was amazed. That's how much blood he had?

'Colvin,' said Mrs Matthews, 'I do not intend to have another fight about this chipper-chopper. If you touch it again, I'm telling you now that you'll be smacked.'

These were grave words, they caused a silence. Colvin dipped his head, but still, out of one eye he could see Lamb Chop happily swinging on the handle of the door. Wait till you're my age, thought Colvin. You won't be happy.

Colvin got his clothes on and zoomed out of his

house with his pockets full of sunflower seeds.

On the way to Lisa's house he saw Justin down the street with his granny. Colvin shouted. 'Justin!'

'Can't come out. I'm going to the barber's.'

'Justin, how many milk bottles of blood have you got in your body?'

Granny gave Justin a tug, she was in a hurry.

'Don't know.'

'Eight!'

Colvin couldn't see Justin's face, but he knew he'd be amazed.

It was half-past nine in the morning, really quite late, but Lisa and Mrs Tomlinson had not yet eaten their breakfast, so they told Colvin he should go on into the living-room and say Hello to Gerry Gerbil.

Queenie was in there, lying in front of the hearth. She stared at Colvin out of two bored, brown eyes.

'Fat Dog,' whispered Colvin, 'fat fat fat fat fat.'

He said all those fats quietly because he did not want Lisa to hear him insulting her dog. 'Rrrrrrrrr.' A low growl happened in Queenie's throat, and Colvin decided to stop calling her fat.

The Tomlinson family kept Gerry Gerbil's cage sitting on a wad of newspapers in a corner of the living-room floor. When Colvin sank to his knees and tinkled the bars, out poked a quivering pink nose and a handsome pair of whiskers.

'I got seeds here, Gerry Gerbil,' Colvin said. 'Millions.'

As he opened the cage door to reach in for the

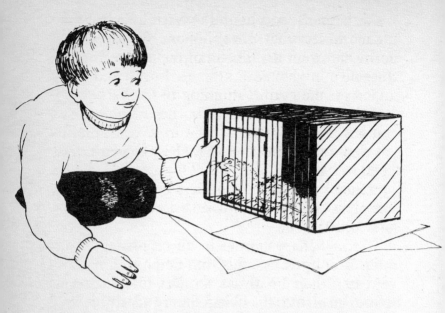

tiny food dish, Colvin made a mistake. He left the cage door open for just a little longer than was wise. Zoom! In no time Gerry Gerbil darted through the gap and scuttled away with his worm of a tail following behind.

Colvin was horrified. 'Come back here, Gerry Gerbil!'

Instead of coming back, that silly gerbil jumped right over Queenie's tail, which made things happen.

'Wuf!' Up jumped Queenie. Astonishment brightened her eyes when they lit on the small, fluffy white thing whizzing about the room.

'Rrrrrr. Wuf wuf wuf. Rrrr-*ruf.*' Queenie whined and yelped and barked at the place where Gerry Gerbil had last been seen running for cover behind the piano.

All that noise was bound to fetch Lisa from the kitchen to see what was going on. She saw Gerry Gerbil run from the far end of the piano. She saw Queenie's mighty leap after it. Both front paws landed on the gerbil, stunning it.

'MUMMMEEEE!'

It was dreadful – there was worse! Mrs Tomlinson flew in flailing a tea-towel at Queenie, but there was no stopping Fat Dog now. Her jaws tightened round the defenceless gerbil, whose tail hung limply down from the dog's mouth.

'Drop it!'

'Mummy, save Gerry Gerbil oh *please*.'

'Drop it Queenie, this minute!'

At last Queenie did as she was told, but even before Lisa ran to pick up Gerry Gerbil it was quite obvious that he was dead.

Lisa said desperately, 'Colvin! Look what you've done, this is the worst thing you've ever done, you ... you are *stupid*. Mummy, little Gerry Gerbil is dead.' And Lisa cried.

Colvin, the guilty one, had turned scarlet. It was no wonder, for his blood was racing round his body, all eight milk bottles full. 'I have to go home now,' he said.

Colvin was sad, Colvin was sorry as he returned wearily to his own house, but he couldn't cry like Lisa, not yet, anyway. He felt so deep-down awful that it didn't seem to matter whether he cried or not, tears would not help.

It wasn't Gerry Gerbil he felt sorry for, it was himself. He would be known as the boy who allowed Miss Lynn's precious gerbil to be zapped by Fat Beast Queenie. Rosy Tea Cosy would talk about this for ever.

In his own house things hadn't changed, he wished he'd stayed there. Beccy was colouring-in, Lamb Chop bashed Slippy Duck on the floor while his mother struggled to change the cylinder of the portable gas fire.

Colvin stood humbly in the middle of the kitchen floor. 'Mummy,' he said, 'I don't want you to shout at me.'

Mrs Matthews, suddenly alert, stopped struggling with the cylinder of the portable gas fire.

'What have you done?'

'Mummy I'm not going to use the chipper-chopper any more.'

Down went Beccy's colouring-in pencil. She wanted to concentrate on listening.

'Colvin,' said Mrs Matthews, 'tell me *now* what you have done.'

'I let Gerry Gerbil out of his cage.'

'And?'

'Queenie zapped him. But it wasn't my fault!'

Beccy's eyes were like circles. 'Oh *Col*-vin. Miss Lynn will faint.'

After too long a time, Mrs Matthews understood at last. She pounced on Lamb Chop and whisked him out of the kitchen, and she had Beccy, still hopeful, following behind, saying, 'But maybe he's not completely dead, Mummy.'

Colvin, left alone, knew better. That gerbil was dead all right, there was nothing deader. I'll have to go to another school, he thought.

Miss Lynn was bound to think he was absolutely useless. She would never wink at him again the way she sometimes did. She would never, never smile for him again.

On Tuesday morning Mrs Matthews did not have a lazy-bones lie-in until nine o'clock. She had some important things to take care of before school started next day, so how could she possibly lie-in? First of all she got up early and ran Mr Matthews to work so that she could have the car at home with her that day.

Colvin and Lisa waited on his front step for Mrs Matthews to return. The empty gerbil cage, wedged between them, was a grim reminder of the events of yesterday. Lisa sighed to see it empty. Poor old Gerry Gerbil, her father had put him in the bin.

But things weren't so bad. Some good plans had been made.

'Do you really think we'll get another one, Colvin? Will we really get another one that looks just the same as our Gerry Gerbil?'

'Yes,' said Colvin, who had no doubts about it. *His* father had said that there were hundreds of Gerry Gerbils.

They were going into town to buy another gerbil and nobody would be able to tell the difference, especially not Rosy Tea Cosy.

Mrs Matthews returned. Lisa and Colvin bundled themselves and the empty gerbil cage into the back seat beside Baby Frederick, who was already strapped into his special safe little seat.

Until a few months ago this had been Colvin's

special safe little seat, so there was another thing he'd given to Lamb Chop recently. I'm very good to my brother, thought Colvin.

The car moved off. They did not zoom, Mrs Matthews never zoomed.

'Mummy,' shouted Colvin, 'does Frederick have eight milk bottles of blood too or would he have only four because he's little?'

'I do not know, Colvin,' said Mrs Matthews impatiently.

Colvin knew that she didn't like driving in the choked-up city traffic with lorries whooshing by on every side, so he and Lisa did some reading practice on the way to the pet shop. They found so many difficult words on the great green signs which spanned the dual carriageways that Colvin was sorry Miss Lynn wasn't with them to say she was pleased.

The car stopped. They had arrived. 'Please let them have gerbils,' said Mrs Matthews.

The pet shop was full of smells when they got inside. Colvin heard birds chirping and he saw a huge white rabbit which blinked at him.

'Mummy, will you buy me a white rabbit?'

'No, Colvin.'

'But that rabbit likes me.'

'No!'

This was disappointing, but Colvin wasn't stupid, he knew that a rabbit wouldn't be safe with Fat Beast living next door. When Queenie got too old to chase things he'd try for a rabbit again.

The lady in charge of the pet shop listened with sympathy while Mrs Matthews went through the whole story – how Gerry Gerbil's escape had been followed by panicking and tears. 'Oh I know,' said the pet shop lady, 'haven't I two of my own!'

Meanwhile, opposite the guinea-pigs and underneath the budgerigars, Colvin and Lisa found exactly what they had come for: two large cages full of cute little jolly gerbils, many with white coats, red eyes, pink tiny ears and tails that looked like worms.

'Over here, Mummy,' cried Colvin. 'Millions of gerbils!'

They were saved. Nothing, on the way home, could fade the smile on Lisa's face. She was happy again.

But one small worry remained. 'Colvin,' she whispered, 'promise you won't tell anybody what happened. We'll not tell anybody this isn't the real Gerry Gerbil, will we? You won't tell Geraldine or Art or Tall Norman? Or Rosalind?'

Did he want Rosy Tea Cosy to find out about Gerry Gerbil? He did not!

'Nobody is going to find out about this,' he said grimly.

As a matter of fact Colvin was quite wrong. Soon, everybody knew about it.

That night Colvin cleaned his teeth in the bathroom and practised gargling water in his throat just like Beccy did. Then he picked up Slippy Duck and headed across the landing towards his bedroom.

He heard his father's voice talking in the hall below. 'Hello? Miss Lynn? This is Colvin's father

here – Colvin Matthews. Yes, that's right. I am very sorry indeed to phone you at home, Miss Lynn.'

Why, Colvin wondered, was his father phoning his teacher? It was such a peculiar thing to happen that he stood still and listened.

'Well, the fact is that we've had a bit of an accident here. No, no, not to Colvin ... I'm afraid he allowed your gerbil to escape and ... Yes. He was very upset, of course. Lisa too. U-huh. We did buy another one, it looks exactly the same but ... Yes of course. Thank you very much, Miss Lynn. I will tell him. Goodnight.'

Mr Matthews stopped talking and set the phone down. Colvin was shocked. Imagine his father telling on him like that! Miss Lynn would know, *everybody* would know.

He took three fierce steps down the stairs. 'What did you tell on me for?' he yelled. 'You want Miss Lynn to be cross with me!'

Mr Matthews was amazed to see Colvin standing on the fifth step up, glaring down at him with tears in his eyes.

'Colvin – I had to tell.'

'You didn't! Nobody would know, they were just the same, they even had the same *whiskers.*'

His father took him firmly by the shoulders. 'Calm down, please. It's not right to fool people, that's what you have to realise, Colvin. Miss Lynn has a right to know that the gerbil you're taking back isn't the same one. It's always better to tell people the truth, they like you better if you do and they don't like being deceived.'

'But Daddy, Daddy, Rosy Tea Cosy...'

'Forget about Rosy Tea Cosy!' his father said loudly.

How, wondered Colvin. He would never forget Rosy Tea Cosy, she was unforgettable.

And yet, in a way, he was relieved that Miss Lynn knew about Gerry Gerbil. Some secrets were fine, but this one had been really big and frightening – he was glad that Miss Lynn knew the worst.

But was she cross with him? He didn't ask, he didn't want to hear.

Mr Matthews scooped Colvin and Slippy Duck up to his shoulder, carried them upstairs and dumped them into bed from a great height.

'Bedtime for all monkeys!' he said. 'Now. I'll have one of those new Neckbreakers before I go.'

Colvin put his arms round his dad's neck and heaved until he heard grunts, but it wasn't a good Neckbreaker.

He was thinking about something else. What would happen tomorrow morning when he and Lisa went to school?

On Wednesday morning when the children of Miss Lynn's class gathered in the playground, there was no sort of a line at all. People were higgledy-piggledy everywhere.

They were listening to Rosalind Cruickshanks, who had some powerful News to tell. She said Gerry Gerbil had been eaten.

Well, little Muy Ling's mouth dropped open wide. Ossie Winchester, on the other hand, licked his lips as if he was hungry for more News. Lisa blushed when Rosalind Cruickshanks pointed at the cheeky little gerbil in the cage.

'That is not the *real* Gerry Gerbil but it wasn't your fault Lisa, Colvin Matthews did it – *he* let Gerry Gerbil die. Art knows, don't you, Art? Lisa's mummy told his mummy, it's really really true.'

Confusion happened. Many people turned to Art to hear more and Colvin, who had come to school that morning with yet another very long sunflower, scowled his absolutely worst scowl at Rosalind Cruickshanks.

She was really looking to be zapped, that Rosy Tea Cosy. If only I wasn't holding my sunflower I might zap her, thought Colvin.

'It wasn't my fault,' he shouted out loudly, 'it was Fat Beast!'

Of course the story had to be told. Colvin made it as exciting as possible, saying how the Fat Beast had trapped Gerry Gerbil with her paws then chewed him up some before help came. While Colvin was amazing his friends with details such as these, Miss Lynn arrived to find her people in a circle instead of a straight line.

'Miss!'

'A dog got Gerry Gerbil!'

'That one's not real, Miss Lynn!'

'Quiet, *please.*'

When, slowly, the clamour died down, Miss Lynn turned to Lisa, who looked thoroughly miserable as she stood there holding the cage and the new gerbil.

Miss Lynn knelt down and whispered to her. 'Wasn't that an awful thing to happen to you, Lisa,' she said. 'But it can't be helped.'

'Miss Lynn, Colvin and me were crying.'

'Well it's all over now, and the new Gerry Gerbil is just lovely. You carry him into class – I'm sure he's going to love school.'

And now Miss Lynn stood up to locate Colvin in her line, which was now, happily, a tidy line. About half-way down a sunflower seemed to be sprouting from the top of Tall Norman's head.

'Colvin. How many of those beautiful flowers have you got?'

'Miss Lynn I've got two more. I cut this one down with my dad's biggest saw, you know.'

His teacher shook her head, her eyes twinkled, she was amazed.

'Well I think you should come to the front of the line and lead the class in this morning, would you do that, please?'

He certainly would. Colvin looked most impressive, a very important person, standing at the front of the line with his sunflower raised like a banner.

Glancing over his shoulder to make sure that the line was straight (*he* wasn't leading a crooked line of people into school), Colvin called out at the top of his voice: 'Right. Ready. Quick march, go!'

Little Muy Ling, Geraldine Elliot, Art, Tall Norman, Lisa with gerbil, Ossie Winchester, Rosy Tea Cosy, the rest of the class, Justin and Miss Lynn followed the bobbing sunflower into school.

MOIRA MILLER

What Size is Andy?

Andy is the middle one of five children –
often too small to play with the bigger
children and too big to behave like the little
ones. But Andy has some special adventures
of his own!

Where Does Andy Go?

'We're going on holiday on a bus!' shouts
Andy to his friend Steve. 'We're going to
live on a bus.'
'Don't believe you!' shouts back Steve.
'Nobody *lives* on a bus.'

But it's true! Andy, Dave, Rosie, Todger,
Mum, Dad and Uncle Billy are off in a real
double-decker bus – for the best holiday
ever!